Whispers in the Shadows

Whispers in the Shadows

A Collection of Chilling Tales

Raven Holloway

Mindful Pages

Published in 2023

ISBN 9789357722551 (eBook)

Published by

Mindful Pages
Imprint of Alpha Editions LLC
312 W. 2nd St #1834
Casper, WY 82601, USA

Contents

The Haunting of Willowbrook Manor

In the heart of the misty countryside stood a decrepit mansion known as Willowbrook Manor. The locals spoke in hushed whispers of the house's dark past and the malevolent spirits that resided within its walls. For years, it remained uninhabited, a place where only the brave—or the foolish—would venture.

One stormy evening, a group of thrill-seekers decided to investigate the rumors surrounding Willowbrook Manor. Among them were Sarah, a daring journalist seeking a captivating story, and James, her skeptical photographer. They were joined by Luke, an adrenaline junkie, and his cautious girlfriend, Emma.

The rain pounded against the car's windows as they drove down the winding road leading to the ominous manor. Lightning streaked across the sky, illuminating the abandoned mansion. Sarah felt a chill crawl up her spine, but she pushed aside her fears, eager to uncover the truth behind the haunted tales.

As they stepped inside, the air turned heavy, suffocating. The creaking floorboards echoed through the house as they explored its shadowy rooms. Sarah's heart raced with every unexplained noise, but she clung to her determination to unravel the mystery.

In the darkness of the living room, the group stumbled upon an old photograph. It depicted a family, their faces twisted in anguish, standing before Willowbrook Manor many years ago. A shiver ran through Sarah as she realized that they looked disturbingly similar to the group she was with.

As they continued their exploration, the atmosphere grew more oppressive. Emma's unease intensified, and Luke tried to reassure her, though his own bravado began to waver. James, the skeptic, couldn't deny the eerie presence surrounding them any longer, and even he began to feel unsettled.

In the heart of the manor, they discovered a locked door. Its wood was decayed, and the brass handle was icy to the touch. Sarah's curiosity got the better of her, and she managed to pick the lock. Inside, they found a room filled with ancient relics and occult symbols adorning the walls.

As the group examined the room, a sudden gust of wind slammed the door shut. Panic seized them, and they tried to open it, but it was stuck fast. In the dim light, they noticed the symbols on the walls seemed to writhe and change, taking on a sinister life of their own.

Sarah felt a hand on her shoulder, and she turned to see a translucent figure looming behind her. The ghostly woman's face contorted into a horrifying visage, and a blood-curdling scream echoed through the house. The others rushed to her aid, but the door remained stubbornly shut.

The apparitions multiplied, each more malevolent than the last. The group was surrounded by a parade of phantoms, each connected to the mansion's chilling history. They were the spirits of a cursed family, their souls forever bound to Willowbrook Manor.

As terror engulfed them, Sarah found herself inexplicably drawn to the photograph she had discovered earlier. The resemblance between her and the woman in the picture was undeniable. The realization hit her like a tidal wave—she was somehow connected to the mansion's tragic past.

In a desperate attempt to break free from the apparitions' grasp, Sarah clutched the photograph tightly and pleaded for the spirits to release them. Slowly, the room's malevolence abated, and the door finally swung open. The spirits receded, fading into the darkness from whence they came.

The group staggered outside, shaken to their core. Sarah and the others had survived the ordeal, but they knew they would never be the same. The haunting of Willowbrook Manor had left an indelible mark on their souls.

Weeks later, Sarah published her account of the harrowing experience at the manor. The story sent shivers down readers' spines and sparked intense debates about the existence of the supernatural. But for Sarah, it was more than just a story—it was a haunting reminder of the thin veil that separated the living from the dead.

Willowbrook Manor remained standing, a silent witness to the darkness it harbored within its walls. Its legend grew, attracting more thrill-seekers and paranormal enthusiasts eager to experience the chilling presence themselves.

But Sarah knew that some mysteries were better left untouched. The horrors she faced that night were beyond comprehension, and she couldn't help but wonder if her destiny had been forever entwined with Willowbrook Manor or if the malevolent spirits that roamed its halls would forever seek new victims.

The Whispering Woods

A thick mist hung over the forest, shrouding the trees in an eerie embrace. The hikers, led by the adventurous Alex, trekked deeper into the ancient woods, their footsteps muffled by the decaying foliage beneath. The air was heavy with an unsettling silence, broken only by faint whispers that seemed to drift from the very heart of the forest.

As dusk settled in, the shadows grew longer, and a chill crept down their spines. The forest seemed to change with the fading light, its branches contorting into twisted forms. Alex urged the group to push forward, eager to uncover the secrets that lay hidden in the heart of the Whispering Woods.

But as night fell, the whispers grew louder, morphing into unintelligible murmurs that made their hairs stand on end. The hikers tried to dismiss their fears, attributing the sounds to the rustling of leaves and the wind through the trees. But deep down, they knew there was something more sinister lurking in the darkness.

As they huddled around their campfire, they exchanged nervous glances. The woods seemed to come alive, with eerie apparitions emerging from the shadows. Vague shapes danced among the trees, their forms indistinct and unsettling. The hikers' hearts pounded in their chests as they realized they were not alone.

The apparitions drew nearer, and one by one, they revealed themselves. Ghostly figures of long-deceased individuals, their faces twisted in agony, moved with unnatural grace through the undergrowth. Some wore tattered clothes from a bygone era, while others appeared more ethereal, almost transparent.

Among the hikers was Maria, a skeptic who had laughed off the stories of the Whispering Woods. But now, her bravado had disappeared, and terror filled her eyes as she faced the haunting specters. Their hollow eyes seemed to pierce through her soul, and she felt a malevolent force drawing her toward them.

In a trembling voice, Maria called out to the others, warning them to flee. But the whispering voices had grown so intense that it was as if the forest itself wanted to keep them trapped within its grasp. The ground trembled beneath their feet as they struggled to escape, but the woods seemed to tighten its hold on them, ensnaring them in its nightmarish web.

As they ran through the tangled underbrush, the forest seemed to stretch on endlessly. Each path they took led them back to the same eerie clearing where the apparitions awaited. It was as if the Whispering Woods had a malevolent intelligence of its own, toying with them and ensuring they would never find their way out.

Terror overwhelmed the hikers, and they clung to each other, praying for a way to break free from the cursed woods. But the whispering voices grew louder, and the apparitions closed in, their twisted forms moving with unnatural swiftness.

Alex, the group's leader, refused to give in to fear. He believed there must be a way to appease the spirits and free them from the forest's grip. With trembling hands, he took out a pendant that had been passed down through generations of his family.

The pendant glowed faintly as Alex chanted ancient incantations he had learned from his grandmother. For a moment, the woods fell silent, and the apparitions seemed to pause, their ethereal forms flickering in the moonlight.

But the moment of respite was short-lived. With a furious howl, the forest erupted into chaos. The apparitions' eyes blazed with wrath, and the ground beneath them churned with a force so powerful it threatened to consume them all.

Maria and the others clung to each other, their screams lost amidst the haunting cacophony. The forest itself seemed to rebel against Alex's attempts to break the curse, and the apparitions closed in, their ghostly fingers reaching out to claim their souls.

As the Whispering Woods swallowed them whole, their cries echoed through the night, but no one beyond the forest would ever hear them again. The ancient woods had claimed its victims, and its malevolent secrets would forever remain hidden, waiting for the next unsuspecting souls to stumble upon its cursed grounds.

The Haunting of Emily's Doll

In the quiet town of Ravenscroft, a family named the Harrisons inherited a house from a distant relative they had never met. Among the belongings left behind was an old, weathered doll named Emily. At first glance, she appeared like any other innocent childhood keepsake, but little did the Harrisons know that Emily held a sinister secret.

The youngest member of the family, Sarah, was immediately drawn to the doll. With her big blue eyes and golden curls, she seemed like the perfect companion for the seven-year-old girl. As Sarah embraced Emily, her parents, John and Elizabeth, exchanged uneasy glances. There was something about the doll that made them uneasy, but they brushed it off as a product of their overactive imaginations.

The first night in the new house, strange occurrences began. Doors creaked open on their own, and cold drafts swept through the rooms, chilling the air. John and Elizabeth tried to reassure each other that it was just an old house settling, but deep down, they couldn't shake the feeling that something was amiss.

In the following days, Sarah's behavior changed. She became withdrawn and would spend hours locked away in her room, whispering to Emily as if they were having secret conversations. The once bubbly and outgoing child now seemed preoccupied and distant, and her parents grew increasingly concerned.

One night, John awoke to the sound of soft giggles echoing through the house. He followed the sound to Sarah's room, where he found her sitting on the floor, surrounded by an eerie glow. The source of the light was Emily, her glassy eyes gleaming with an unnatural brightness.

"S-Sarah?" John stammered, his heart pounding. "What are you doing?"

Sarah looked up, her eyes vacant as if she were in a trance. "Emily wants to play, Daddy. She says we're going to have so much fun."

John reached out to take the doll away, but the moment his hand touched Emily, an icy sensation shot through his entire body. He recoiled in horror as the giggles grew louder, echoing through the room.

In the days that followed, Elizabeth noticed changes in the house's atmosphere. The walls seemed to weep, and the air felt heavy with an unsettling presence. Objects moved on their own, and eerie whispers filled the hallways, making her skin crawl.

Desperate for answers, Elizabeth began researching the doll's origins. She discovered that Emily had once belonged to a young girl who tragically died under mysterious circumstances. The doll had been found at the scene, but it disappeared shortly after the girl's death, only to resurface in the Harrison's inheritance.

Terrified by the revelation, Elizabeth confronted Sarah about the doll. Tears welled up in Sarah's eyes as she confessed that Emily wasn't just a doll; she was her only friend in the house.

"I didn't mean to make her angry, Mommy," Sarah sobbed. "But when I'm sad, she talks to me, and I feel better. She doesn't like it when you and Daddy get mad at her."

Elizabeth's heart broke for her daughter, but she knew they had to get rid of the doll. She contacted a local paranormal expert, Mr. Sinclair, to help them cleanse the house of Emily's sinister presence.

As Mr. Sinclair arrived, he sensed the malevolence that lingered in the doll. He explained to the Harrisons that the spirit of the deceased girl had attached itself to Emily, seeking solace and companionship in the living world.

In the dimly lit living room, Mr. Sinclair performed a cleansing ritual, calling upon the spirits to release Emily's hold on the family. But as he chanted, the lights flickered, and a low growl reverberated through the room. It was as if the spirit within the doll resisted being banished.

Undeterred, Mr. Sinclair pressed on, urging the spirit to find peace and move on. As he chanted, the temperature in the room plummeted, and a sinister voice filled the air, speaking in a language unknown to the living.

In the midst of the chaos, the doll began to levitate, its eyes now glowing with a fiery intensity. The Harrisons watched in horror as the spirit manifested itself before them, its form shifting between the doll and the ghostly figure of a young girl.

"Leave us alone!" Mr. Sinclair commanded. "You do not belong in this world. Find your peace and let go!"

But the spirit's rage intensified, and the haunting presence grew stronger. The room trembled, and Sarah clung to her parents, fear etched on her face.

"Please," Elizabeth pleaded. "We mean you no harm. Find your way to the light and leave us in peace."

For a moment, the spirit wavered, torn between its attachment to the living world and the afterlife. And then, with a final burst of energy, it seemed to dissipate into the air, leaving Emily the doll lifeless and still.

The room fell silent, and the oppressive atmosphere lifted. The house felt peaceful once more, as if the evil presence had finally departed.

Days turned into weeks, and the Harrisons settled into their new home without the looming terror of Emily's haunting. Sarah's spirits lifted, and she started making new friends at school. The memories of the sinister doll began to fade, and they hoped to leave the nightmare behind them.

But little did they know that in the attic, tucked away in an old box, Emily the doll had found a new home, biding her time for another chance to unleash her malevolence upon an unsuspecting soul. The sinister secret she held would continue to haunt whoever dared cross her path, forever seeking solace in the living world.

Reflections of the Damned

In the heart of the quaint town of Greenwood, Emily, a young woman seeking a fresh start, moved into a centuries-old house that had stood vacant for years. Among the antiques and relics left behind, an ornate mirror caught her eye. Its gilded frame exuded an air of grandeur, and Emily couldn't resist the allure of owning a piece of history.

As she hung the mirror in her bedroom, a shiver ran down her spine. She attributed it to the excitement of her new home and dismissed any lingering unease. But as the days passed, Emily couldn't shake the feeling that something was off. Each time she glanced into the mirror, a flicker of uncertainty passed over her reflection's face.

One night, as the moon cast an eerie glow through her window, Emily gazed into the mirror and gasped. Her reflection smiled back, but there was a malevolent glint in its eyes. The room seemed to grow colder as Emily stumbled backward, her heart pounding in her chest.

She chided herself for imagining things and blamed the unsettling sensation on the late hour. But as the days turned into weeks, the mirror's reflections grew more unsettling. Emily would see herself weeping, even when she felt no tears on her cheeks. Her reflection would smirk, as if mocking her, when she was filled with joy.

Haunted by the twisted versions of her reality, Emily sought solace from her friends, who brushed off her concerns as stress-induced hallucinations. Even her therapist dismissed it as her mind playing tricks on her.

Determined to prove her sanity, Emily decided to document the mirror's reflections. Each time she saw something strange, she captured it on her phone. But when she showed the images to others, the mirror's devious reflections were nowhere to be found.

Confused and desperate for answers, Emily delved into the history of the mirror. She discovered that it had once belonged to a powerful family known for dabbling in the dark arts. Legends spoke of a malevolent entity trapped within the mirror, condemned to prey upon its owners and twist their realities.

Fear gnawed at Emily's mind, but a part of her refused to accept that a malevolent spirit lurked within the mirror. She continued living in the house, hoping to disprove the haunting rumors.

One night, as Emily lay in bed, she heard soft whispers coming from the mirror. The words were unintelligible, but the sinister tone sent shivers down her spine. The mirror's surface rippled, and a grotesque version of Emily emerged from within, her face contorted into a nightmarish grin.

"You're mine now," the doppelgänger sneered, her voice a twisted mockery of Emily's own.

Paralyzed with fear, Emily watched as her reflection stepped out of the mirror and into the room. The doppelgänger approached the bed, its fingers trailing along the sheets, leaving a trail of frost in their wake.

"You can't escape me," the reflection taunted. "I am a part of you now, and there's no running from your own darkness."

Emily's heart raced as she tried to gather her courage. "No," she whispered, her voice trembling. "I won't let you control me."

The doppelgänger let out a chilling laugh, causing the walls to reverberate with its malevolence. "You can't fight what's inside you," it hissed. "The mirror merely shows you the truth, the darkness that lies dormant in your soul."

Tears welled up in Emily's eyes as she struggled to break free from the mirror's grasp. She refused to accept the doppelgänger's words, knowing that she was more than her darkest thoughts.

With every ounce of strength, Emily lunged forward and plunged her hand into the mirror. The surface felt icy cold, but she could feel an energy coursing through her fingertips, connecting her to the malevolent entity within.

In a desperate act of defiance, Emily chanted a spell she had found in her research, a banishment incantation meant to rid the mirror of its cursed inhabitant. The mirror trembled, and the doppelgänger let out an ear-piercing shriek as it was pulled back into the depths of the glass.

The mirror's surface settled, and Emily collapsed to the floor, gasping for breath. She had faced her darkest fears and banished the malevolent spirit that had sought to consume her.

As dawn broke, Emily decided to get rid of the mirror, fearing that it might find its way back into her life. She contacted a group of paranormal experts who specialized in dealing with cursed objects. Together, they sealed the mirror in a vault lined with protective wards, ensuring that its malevolence could never harm anyone again.

In the days that followed, Emily found peace and solace, no longer tormented by the mirror's reflections. She embraced the light within her and learned to accept the complexities of her own being.

But even as she moved forward, she couldn't forget the twisted version of herself she had seen in the mirror. Emily knew that the darkness would always linger within her, but she vowed never to let it consume her soul. She had survived the horrors of the mirror's reflection and emerged stronger, determined to face any darkness that lay ahead.

The Haunting Carousel

In the small town of Briarwood, there stood an abandoned amusement park known as Joyland. Once a bustling attraction that brought joy to families, it now lay in decay, its rides and attractions weathered by time and neglect. Legend had it that the park was cursed, haunted by the spirits of those who had lost their lives there in a tragic accident years ago.

A group of curious teenagers, seeking a thrill and eager to test their bravery, gathered on a moonlit night at the gates of Joyland. Their eyes sparkled with a mix of excitement and trepidation as they prepared to venture into the forgotten realm.

Leading the group was Jake, a daredevil with a mischievous grin. He had heard the stories of the park's curse but dismissed them as mere urban legends. Alongside him were Mia, a fearless girl with an adventurous spirit, and her cautious best friend, Sam. Rounding out the group were Lily, the skeptic, and Ben, a thrill-seeker drawn to the eerie allure of the abandoned amusement park.

As they stepped through the rusty gates, a chill wind whispered through the air, and the distant sound of creaking rides filled their ears. Moonlight cast eerie shadows on the dilapidated structures, heightening the sense of foreboding that hung heavy in the atmosphere.

Their first stop was the Ferris wheel, its once vibrant colors now faded and peeling. As they climbed into the rickety carts, a cold gust of wind blew, causing the wheel to creak to life.

Slowly, it ascended into the night sky, carrying the teens towards the stars.

But as they reached the pinnacle, a shroud of darkness enveloped them. The laughter of children echoed through the wind, mingling with the pained screams of those who had met their fate in this place. Panic surged through their veins as the Ferris wheel spun out of control, swaying perilously as if guided by an unseen force.

With a jolt, the Ferris wheel came to a halt, leaving the teenagers stranded at the top. Their terrified screams were drowned out by the ghostly voices, their desperate pleas for salvation blending with the haunting melody of the park's past.

After what felt like an eternity, the wheel started moving again, descending slowly to the ground. Trembling and pale, the group stumbled out of the carts, their minds reeling from the harrowing experience. But their curiosity remained unsatiated, pushing them deeper into the heart of Joyland.

Their next destination was the haunted house, its facade crumbling and covered in ivy. The creaking front door beckoned them, and with a shared glance, they stepped inside, plunging into darkness. Shadows danced on the walls as their footsteps echoed through the empty corridors.

Whispers filled the air, chilling their spines. Ghostly apparitions materialized before them, their faces contorted in pain. The spirits of those who had perished in the fire that engulfed the haunted house long ago sought to communicate their anguish.

Amidst the chaos, Lily's skepticism crumbled. Fear etched across her face, she realized that the legends were true. The curse of Joyland was real, and they were trapped in its clutches.

Driven by a mix of fear and determination, the group pressed on, determined to find a way out. But as they navigated the crumbling pathways, they stumbled upon the park's main attraction, the grand carousel.

Its painted horses, now faded and chipped, moved in a haunting rhythm. The organ music played, a melancholic melody that seemed to echo through the ages. Transfixed, they watched as the carousel spun faster and faster, its lights flickering with an otherworldly glow.

As if pulled by an unseen force, Mia reached out to touch one of the carousel horses. But as her fingers made contact, an agonizing scream filled the air, and the other horses came to life. They twisted and contorted, their eyes glowing with malevolence.

Terrified, the group tried to flee, but the carousel held them in place, its spellbinding magic too strong to resist. Mia's hand was stuck, and her screams merged with the ghostly wails that echoed through the park.

A chilling figure emerged from the center of the carousel, a spirit trapped in perpetual agony. Its eyes locked with theirs, and they felt an overwhelming sense of sorrow and despair.

"You should not have come here," the ghostly figure whispered, its voice a hollow echo of the past. "Leave now, while you still can."

Their hearts pounding, the teenagers managed to break free from the carousel's hold. Without a second thought, they ran, leaving behind the malevolent spirits that roamed Joyland.

Back at the gates, they glanced back one last time at the forsaken amusement park. In the moonlit darkness, the ghostly figures danced among the ruins, forever bound to their tragic past.

As they walked away, the whispers of the cursed park still lingered in their ears, a haunting reminder of the night they dared to enter the forgotten realm of Joyland. The curse of the amusement park would forever haunt their memories, a chilling tale to be passed down through generations, warning others of the malevolent spirits that lurked within the abandoned rides and attractions of Joyland.

The Haunting Ring

In the peaceful town of Ravenwood, the nights were often quiet, save for the occasional hooting of an owl or the rustling of leaves in the wind. But everything changed when the phantom caller began to strike.

It started innocently enough – a few strange phone calls to random residents, their voices distorted and eerie. The callers would predict seemingly trivial events like a broken window or a power outage. At first, people dismissed them as pranks or coincidences, but soon, the calls took a darker turn.

One fateful night, a chilling voice whispered through the receiver, "Beware the river's edge tonight, for the waters will claim a soul." The call ended abruptly, leaving the recipient trembling with fear. The next day, news spread of a tragic accident by the river – a young boy had drowned, just as the caller had predicted.

Fear swept through the town like wildfire. No one knew who was behind the calls, and each ring of the phone became a source of terror. The police launched a thorough investigation, but the phantom caller seemed to leave no traces, no clues to their identity.

As the days turned into weeks, the calls continued, each prophecy more unsettling than the last. People started to suspect their friends, their neighbors, even their own family members. Trust in the tight-knit community began to erode, replaced by fear and suspicion.

One night, the phone rang in the home of Emma Turner, a young woman living alone. Her heart raced as she picked up the receiver, dreading what the caller might say this time.

"The old oak tree on Elm Street will fall tonight, and death shall follow," the chilling voice declared.

Emma's hands trembled, and she hung up the phone. She tried to shrug off the fear and convince herself that it was just a sick prank, but a nagging unease lingered. Unable to ignore the call, she decided to take a walk to the old oak tree, hoping to dispel her fears by facing them head-on.

The moon shone brightly overhead as Emma approached the tree. Its gnarled branches loomed overhead, casting eerie shadows on the ground. Her heart pounded in her chest, and she contemplated turning back, but a strange compulsion urged her to stay.

As if in slow motion, the ancient oak began to creak, its roots groaning under the weight of the centuries-old tree. With a deafening crash, the massive tree fell, just as the caller had predicted.

Emma's breath caught in her throat as she heard a cry of pain in the distance. Rushing towards the sound, she discovered her elderly neighbor trapped beneath the fallen oak. She called for help, and together with other concerned residents, they managed to free him. But it was too late – he had suffered a fatal injury.

The tragic event left the town in shock. The phantom caller's predictions had come true once more, leaving no room for doubt or disbelief. The terror escalated, and the town descended into chaos.

In a desperate attempt to put an end to the torment, the townspeople organized a community meeting. The atmosphere was tense, and accusations flew like daggers. Every face held a glimmer of suspicion as they searched for the one responsible for the calls.

As the meeting reached a crescendo of anxiety, a stranger entered the room. Dressed in a dark coat and a wide-brimmed hat that shadowed his face, he introduced himself as Mr. Hawthorne, a paranormal investigator.

"I've been tracking the source of these calls," he said, his voice low and enigmatic. "There is a malevolent force at play here, and I believe it is not of this world."

The room fell silent as Mr. Hawthorne explained that the calls were not merely pranks but a sinister manifestation of a vengeful spirit. Decades ago, an innocent person had been wrongfully accused and sentenced to death, and now their restless soul sought revenge on Ravenwood.

Determined to put an end to the curse, the townspeople rallied behind Mr. Hawthorne. They followed his guidance and performed a ritual to cleanse the town of the malevolent spirit's influence.

With each toll of the clock at midnight, the phantom calls ceased, and peace returned to Ravenwood. The residents began to rebuild their fractured community, holding on to the lessons learned during the harrowing ordeal.

But even as the darkness lifted, the memory of the phantom caller lingered, a haunting reminder of the thin line between the living and the dead. The small town of Ravenwood would never forget the chilling prophecy of the phantom caller, a tale that would echo through generations, a cautionary reminder of the consequences of past injustices left unresolved.

The Elegy of Despair

In the heart of a small, forgotten town, lived a talented but struggling musician named Sarah. One day, as she explored the dusty attic of her old house, she stumbled upon an ancient manuscript hidden amongst a pile of forgotten belongings. The pages were yellowed with age, and the ink had faded, but the musical notations were clear and mysterious.

Intrigued, Sarah brushed off the cobwebs and brought the manuscript down to her piano. As she played the haunting melody, the air seemed to grow colder, and an unsettling feeling washed over her. The notes resonated with a melancholic despair, as if they carried the weight of a sorrowful past.

Unbeknownst to Sarah, the musical composition she had discovered was cursed, a forbidden elegy composed long ago by a tormented soul seeking to trap its pain and suffering within the notes. As Sarah continued to play, the vengeful spirit of the composer awakened, drawn to the sounds of its sorrowful creation.

Night after night, Sarah found herself haunted by eerie occurrences. The once soothing music now filled her dreams, transforming them into nightmares of a ghostly figure shrouded in darkness, reaching out for her with spectral hands. Strange shadows danced across her walls, and objects moved inexplicably.

Frightened and desperate for answers, Sarah sought the help of an elderly town historian, Mr. Thompson. With trepidation in his eyes, he listened to Sarah's tale and revealed the dark history of the manuscript she had unwittingly unleashed.

"It is said that the composer of that elegy was a troubled soul named Eliza," Mr. Thompson began, his voice hushed with caution. "Her heart was broken, and her life was filled with tragedy. She poured her pain into that composition, sealing her suffering within its notes. But in doing so, she inadvertently bound her spirit to the music, cursing anyone who dared to play it."

Determined to break the curse and find peace for both Eliza's tormented soul and her own, Sarah embarked on a quest to uncover the truth behind the tragedy that had led to the creation of the haunting melody.

Through dusty archives and long-forgotten journals, Sarah pieced together the fragments of Eliza's life. She discovered that Eliza had been a gifted musician herself, but her talent had been overshadowed by her sister, Amelia, who was celebrated as the town's musical prodigy.

Fueled by jealousy and despair, Eliza had composed the cursed elegy as a desperate cry for recognition. But when Amelia fell gravely ill, Eliza's grief and remorse overwhelmed her, and she blamed herself for her sister's suffering.

The more Sarah delved into the past, the stronger the vengeful spirit's presence became. The ghostly figure that had haunted her dreams now manifested itself in the waking world, lurking in the shadows, its mournful wails echoing through the house.

As Sarah drew closer to the truth, Eliza's spirit grew increasingly agitated, tormenting her relentlessly. The haunting melody followed her everywhere, and Sarah's sanity began to fray under the weight of the curse.

In a last-ditch effort to confront the vengeful spirit, Sarah decided to perform the elegy in public, hoping to release Eliza's trapped soul and break the curse once and for all.

As the night of the performance arrived, Sarah's heart pounded with both fear and determination. The concert hall was filled with an eerie stillness as she played the cursed elegy on the grand piano.

The haunting melody filled the air, and Sarah could feel the presence of Eliza's spirit growing stronger with every note. But she pressed on, pouring her heart and soul into the music, hoping to bring closure to the tormented soul of the composer.

Suddenly, the temperature in the hall plummeted, and a cold wind swirled around Sarah. The vengeful spirit materialized before her, its face contorted with anguish and anger.

But as Sarah continued to play, the ghostly figure began to change. The anger in its eyes softened, and tears streamed down its translucent cheeks. Eliza's spirit seemed to be releasing the pain it had carried for so long.

Through the haunting melody, Sarah could feel a sense of forgiveness and release emanating from Eliza's spirit. The curse was finally being lifted, and the vengeful pursuit ceased.

The last notes of the elegy faded into the silence of the concert hall. The ghostly figure of Eliza vanished, leaving behind a sense of peace that permeated the space.

From that moment on, the cursed manuscript held no power over Sarah. The haunting melody was no longer a source of terror but a testament to the enduring power of music and the capacity for redemption and forgiveness.

Sarah's life returned to a semblance of normalcy, but she never forgot the haunting journey she had undertaken. She continued to play the piano, now composing her own music filled with hope and healing.

And in the attic of her old house, the cursed manuscript rested in a locked box, a silent reminder of the darkness that could be unleashed by a melody steeped in sorrow and revenge.

The Enigmatic Abode

In the heart of the dense forest, hidden away from the modern world, lay a village seemingly forgotten by time. Its name was whispered only in hushed tones by those who dared speak of it at all - Hauntridge. Urban legends painted it as a cursed place, a village that vanished into the mist, never to be seen again. But for a group of thrill-seeking urban explorers, the tales of Hauntridge held a magnetic pull.

Curiosity brimming in their eyes, four friends - Alex, Sarah, Mark, and Emily - set out on a journey to find the elusive village. Armed with backpacks, flashlights, and a determination to uncover the truth, they ventured deep into the heart of the forest.

As they trekked through the tangled undergrowth, they could feel an eerie sensation in the air, as though the forest itself was watching and warning them to turn back. But their excitement was too strong, and they pressed on.

Finally, after hours of walking, they stumbled upon an ancient stone archway, overgrown with vines and moss. Beyond it lay the forgotten village of Hauntridge. The sight that greeted them sent shivers down their spines.

The village appeared untouched by time, frozen in a bygone era. Dilapidated cottages stood like silent sentinels, their windows boarded up, and their doors barely hanging on their hinges. The air was heavy with a sense of desolation, as if the village itself mourned its fate.

Intrigued by the mystery, the explorers split up to investigate the village's secrets. Sarah and Emily ventured into the crumbling church, while Alex and Mark wandered towards an old well in the village center.

As the explorers delved deeper into the village's history, they found fragments of a dark past. The church walls were adorned with cryptic symbols, and faded scriptures hinted at rituals performed long ago. The well, they discovered, was not just a source of water but had been the site of grim sacrifices.

As night fell, a haunting melody began to emanate from the depths of the forest, sending chills down their spines. Sarah clutched her ears, trying to block out the eerie sound, but it seemed to echo in their minds, pulling them closer to the village's dark secrets.

In their attempts to escape the haunting melody, the group found themselves trapped within Hauntridge's cursed confines. The stone archway that had once led them in now refused to let them leave. Panic set in, and they realized they were bound to the village's fate.

Desperate to break free from the village's clutches, they sought refuge in the decrepit church, where the haunting melody seemed less pronounced. As they huddled together, they noticed an ancient journal hidden amidst the debris.

In trembling hands, Sarah opened the journal and began to read. The words told a tale of a village once prosperous, where the people thrived under the protection of a malevolent entity known as the "Harbinger of Shadows."

The Harbinger was appeased through sinister rituals and offerings, ensuring the village's prosperity at the cost of innocent lives. But as the villagers' guilt and fear grew, they decided to rebel against the Harbinger's demands, sealing its wrath in the village forever.

The journal spoke of a chilling ritual that bound the souls of the villagers to the village, forever shackled to the Harbinger's will. Reading further, they realized that the haunting melody they heard was the lament of the trapped souls, forever cursed to sing their anguish.

As the night wore on, the haunting melody grew louder and more intense, threatening to drive them to madness. The spirits of the villagers began to manifest, their faces twisted in eternal agony.

The group knew they had to find a way to break the curse before they, too, became part of the spectral ensemble. Guided by the journal's cryptic instructions, they gathered what little strength remained within them and began to reenact the long-forgotten ritual that had sealed Hauntridge's fate.

They lit candles, drew symbols on the church floor, and chanted ancient incantations. With each passing moment, the melody waned, and the village trembled as if resisting their efforts to break free from its grasp.

As dawn approached, the ritual reached its climax. The ground beneath them rumbled, and the stone archway began to crack. The Harbinger's grip on the village was weakening.

With one final burst of determination, they channeled their energy into the ritual, and a blinding light enveloped the village. The ancient curse began to unravel, and the spirits of the villagers slowly faded away into the ether.

As the sun rose on the horizon, the forest around Hauntridge seemed to sigh with relief. The village was no longer frozen in time; its hold over the explorers had loosened.

Alex, Sarah, Mark, and Emily stepped out of the village, their bodies exhausted, but their spirits freed. The haunting melody had ceased, and they knew the village of Hauntridge would now be forgotten by time once more.

But as they walked away, the group couldn't help but feel a lingering presence. The memory of Hauntridge, with its cursed secrets and mournful souls, would forever haunt their dreams, a chilling reminder that some mysteries are best left untouched, and some melodies should never be played.

The Carnival of Shadows

The arrival of the traveling circus brought both excitement and curiosity to the small town of Greenwood. The carnival grounds were filled with colorful tents, whimsical rides, and mesmerizing performances that promised delights and thrills beyond imagination. But as the townspeople attended the grand opening, they couldn't shake off the unsettling feeling that something was amiss.

A peculiar mist seemed to shroud the carnival, and the moon barely peeked through the heavy clouds that gathered overhead. The performers, dressed in elaborate costumes, moved with an unnatural grace, their smiles hiding something sinister beneath. The townspeople whispered to each other about the eerie ambiance, but their curiosity kept them from leaving.

Among the carnival-goers was a curious young woman named Emma, drawn to the carnival like a moth to a flame. She felt an inexplicable connection to the carnival, as though an invisible force was pulling her towards it. Ignoring the unease creeping up her spine, she wandered deeper into the heart of the sinister carnival.

Emma found herself entranced by the eerie beauty of the sideshow attractions. There was the fortune-teller, Madame Zara, who stared at her with knowing eyes, and the illusionist, Mr. Elysium, who could make objects disappear and reappear at will. Each performer seemed to possess a power that went beyond mere entertainment.

As the night wore on, the carnival's atmosphere grew darker. The townspeople who attended the performances began to vanish without a trace, leaving behind only whispers and memories. Fear gripped the hearts of those who remained, but they couldn't tear themselves away from the haunting allure of the carnival.

Emma's friend, Ethan, had been among the missing. She felt an urgent need to find him, to rescue him from whatever malevolent force had swallowed him whole. Against her better judgment, she sought the help of Madame Zara, the enigmatic fortune-teller.

Inside her dimly lit tent, Madame Zara gazed into a crystal ball, her eyes glinting with an otherworldly light. She warned Emma of the sinister carnival's true nature, a place where lost souls were trapped and consumed to feed the performers' insatiable hunger for power.

Emma's heart pounded, and she demanded to know how to save her friend. Madame Zara handed her an old, weathered book, containing a ritual to break the carnival's curse and free the trapped souls.

Armed with determination and the ancient knowledge, Emma ventured further into the heart of the carnival, avoiding the performers who seemed to watch her every move with malicious intent.

As she delved deeper, the carnival transformed around her. The rides became twisted versions of themselves, creaking and groaning with malevolence. The laughter of children echoed through the air, but the sound was haunting, as if it was the mocking cry of lost souls.

Emma finally found herself in a forbidden area, hidden from the prying eyes of the crowd. There stood the Ringmaster's tent, surrounded by an aura of darkness and foreboding.

Summoning her courage, Emma stepped inside, and there, sitting on a grand throne, was the Ringmaster - a tall, gaunt figure with piercing eyes that seemed to see into her soul.

"You shouldn't have come here, child," the Ringmaster said, his voice a chilling whisper.

"I'm here to free my friend and put an end to this curse," Emma replied, clutching the book tightly in her trembling hands.

The Ringmaster's laughter sent shivers down her spine. "You cannot break the curse," he said. "The sinister carnival feeds on the souls of the lost, and once you're here, you can never leave."

Emma refused to back down, reciting the words of the ritual with unwavering determination. The Ringmaster's expression twisted with rage as he tried to stop her, but Emma persisted.

The ground trembled beneath them, and the sinister carnival seemed to come alive with malevolent energy. The performers emerged from the shadows, their true forms revealed - grotesque and demonic entities, hungry for the souls of the living.

With every word of the ritual, the carnival's grip on the lost souls weakened. The darkness that shrouded the carnival grounds began to dissipate, and the trapped townspeople appeared, their faces etched with despair and pleading for salvation.

Finally, as Emma uttered the last words of the ritual, a blinding light engulfed the carnival, and a deafening roar filled the air. The malevolent entities screamed in agony as their power was stripped away, and the carnival itself began to collapse.

Emma felt an overwhelming surge of energy as she absorbed the curse into herself. With a final burst of strength, she broke free from the carnival's grasp, pulling her friend Ethan and the other lost souls with her.

As the last echoes of the sinister carnival faded, Emma and the rescued townspeople found themselves outside the carnival grounds, the circus now nothing more than a distant memory.

From that day on, the small town of Greenwood prospered, and the sinister carnival was forgotten. But Emma knew that the darkness still lurked, waiting for an opportunity to return.

With the ancient book in her possession, Emma vowed to protect her town and keep the sinister carnival at bay, ever watchful for any signs of its ominous return. She had faced the malevolent power and emerged victorious, but she understood that evil could never truly be destroyed - only contained, for now.

The Haunting of Hollowbrook House

The Hollowbrook House stood nestled on the outskirts of town, a relic of a forgotten era. For years, the locals had whispered chilling tales about the locked basement door that no one dared to open. The house had remained vacant for decades, and its dark history was etched into the minds of the townspeople.

When the Myers family moved to town, they were drawn to the charm of Hollowbrook House. John, a history enthusiast, saw the old house as a chance to immerse himself in the past. His wife, Margaret, fell in love with the sprawling garden and the promise of a peaceful life for their two children, Emma and Tommy.

As the family settled into their new home, they couldn't ignore the eerie feeling that seemed to permeate the air. The neighbors warned them about the locked basement door, cautioning them not to disturb whatever malevolent force lurked behind it. But John dismissed the stories as mere superstitions, determined to prove that there was nothing amiss.

One fateful evening, while John was away at work, a curious Tommy, the youngest of the Myers children, found himself in front of the mysterious basement door. It beckoned to him, its rusted lock almost daring him to open it.

Against his better judgment, Tommy found an old key in the dusty drawer of a nearby cabinet. With trembling hands, he inserted the key into the lock, and with a click, the basement door creaked open.

A chill swept through the house as if the very foundations trembled with dread. Tommy felt a sense of foreboding, but before he could shut the door, an unseen force pushed him forward, sending him tumbling down the basement stairs.

From that moment, an ominous presence seemed to awaken within the house. The air grew colder, and strange occurrences plagued the Myers family. Doors slammed shut on their own, and unsettling whispers echoed through the halls at night.

Margaret began to suffer from unexplained bruises that appeared on her arms as if she had been gripped by invisible hands. Emma, once cheerful and outgoing, became withdrawn and started seeing shadowy figures lurking in the corners of her vision.

John, the skeptic, could no longer ignore the chilling reality of their situation. Desperate to protect his family, he researched the history of Hollowbrook House and discovered a long-buried secret.

Decades ago, the house belonged to the sinister Blackwood family, rumored to be practitioners of dark arts. They were banished from the town after being accused of a heinous crime the sacrifice of innocent souls to attain immortality. The basement door had been locked to seal away the malevolent force that the Blackwoods had unleashed upon the world.

The Myers family had unwittingly unleashed that very force, and it was seeking revenge for the ancient wrongs done to it.

With the help of a local historian, John learned that the malevolent entity could only be contained by the same ritual that had sealed it away in the first place. They needed to gather the remains of the souls that had been sacrificed and return them to the basement, along with a sacred incantation to imprison the malevolent force once more.

But as the haunting intensified, time seemed to slip away, and the malevolent force grew stronger, feeding off the fear and anguish of the Myers family.

One night, when the malevolent entity's wrath reached a crescendo, John decided there was no more time to waste. Armed with the sacred ritual, he led his family down into the depths of the basement, facing the terror that awaited them.

The basement was a sinister place, filled with relics of the Blackwood family's dark practices. In the flickering candlelight, the Myers family began the ritual, their voices quivering with fear and determination.

As they recited the incantation, the malevolent force manifested itself, taking on a terrifying form that defied description. It shrieked and howled, lashing out at them with ghostly tendrils.

But the Myers family stood firm, holding onto the memories of their love and the life they had built together. With every word of the incantation, the entity weakened, its grip on the family loosening.

With a final surge of energy, the Myers family placed the remains of the sacrificed souls in a circle around the malevolent force and completed the ritual.

In a blinding flash of light, the malevolent entity was sucked back into the depths of the basement, the door slamming shut and locking itself once again.

The house fell silent, and the chilling presence that had tormented the family was finally gone.

The Myers family knew that the malevolent force could never truly be destroyed, but they had succeeded in containing it once more.

As they left the basement and returned to the warmth and safety of their home, they knew they would never forget the horrors they had faced within the walls of Hollowbrook House. But they also knew that they had faced those horrors together and emerged stronger than ever.

From that day on, the basement door remained locked, a silent sentinel guarding the malevolent force within.

And though the stories of Hollowbrook House continued to be whispered among the townspeople, the Myers family knew the true horrors that lurked behind that door, a secret they would carry with them for the rest of their lives.

About Raven Holloway

-38-

Raven Holloway is an enigmatic wordsmith whose haunting tales have left readers spellbound in the realm of horror and the supernatural. With a penchant for the macabre and an uncanny ability to infuse every word with an eerie atmosphere, Raven has become a prominent figure in the world of dark fiction.

Hailing from the shadows, Raven's true identity remains shrouded in mystery, adding an extra layer of allure to their already chilling stories. Their pen name perfectly reflects the haunting themes that permeate their works, with each tale unfolding like a dance between the living and the dead.